All Together NOW!

Whoosh around the Mulberry Bush

If you're happy and you know it!

Doing the Animal BOP

Jan Ormerod

OXFORD
UNIVERSITY PRESS

Lindsey Gardiner

This book takes its inspiration from the much-loved song 'Here We Go Round the Mulberry Bush': the words can be sung to the same rhythm and there are animal noises and actions, too. It's a book that invites lots of high-energy enjoyment but it's also a book that can be shared with young children to talk about habitats around the world, encouraging them to develop an awareness of the great diversity of wildlife that our planet supports.

Whoosh
around the
Mulberry
Bush

Here we go round the mulberry bush, with a mulberry whoosh and a mulberry swoosh.

Here we go round the mulberry bush on a **COLD** and **frosty** morning.

This is the way we slime along,
flippety flap and sing a song.

Here we go round the **flower bed** on a sweetly smelling morning.

This is the way we **dig** and **dive**, **scuttle** and **crawl**, **nip** and **pinch**.

Here we go round the
sandy shore
on a breezy summer morning.

This is the way we **flip** our fins,
swim and **SWOOP**,
dart and dive.

Here we go round the deep blue sea on a salty bubbly morning.

This is the way we **YIP YIP YIP,** Sneak and Slink, woo woo woo.

Here we go round the **tumbleweed**

On a **scorching** desert morning.

This is the way we clack and call, slither and squeeze, scream and swing.

This is the way we **suck** and **slurp**, **wallow** in mud, **kick** our heels.

Here we go round the waterhole on a **dry** and **dusty** morning.

This is the way we **slap** and **clap**, **slip** and **slide**, splish and splash.

Here we go round the **icicle** on a **sparkling** snowy morning.

This is the way we Croaky Croak, leap and jump, hop and flop.

Here we go round the mossy log on a misty moisty morning.

This is the way we **flit** and **fly,** **swoop** and **soar,** big eyes **wide.**

Here we go round the starry night just before the morning.

Let's all do the mulberry whoosh and mulberry swoosh around that bush!

Let's all do the **mulberry whoosh** every single morning!

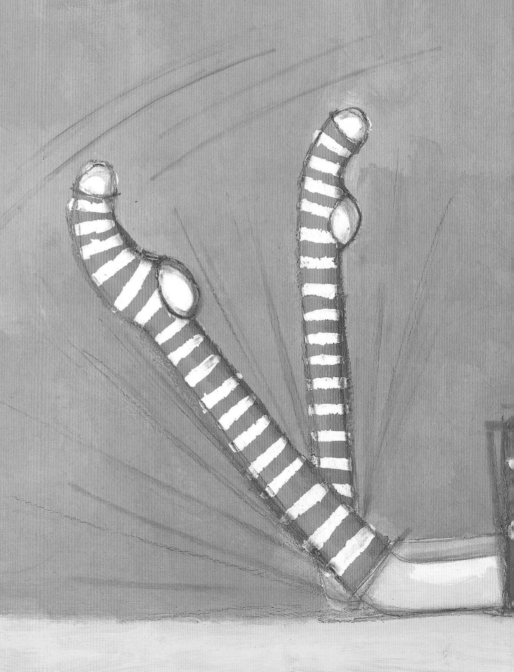

Children everywhere know and love the rhyme 'If You're Happy and You Know It!' – it's great fun to join in the familiar actions of clapping hands and stamping feet. But in this version children can discover how different animals would enjoy the rhyme in their own unique ways. The animals range from a familiar brown dog to more exotic toucans and hyenas. And they're all different to us, so talk about what makes them different: trunks, beaks, tails, wings, claws, fur, feathers, and so on.

If you're happy and you know it!

One day a little girl felt

'If you're happy and you know it, clap your hands.

If you're happy and you know it,
clap your hands –

If you're happy and you know it,
clap your hands –

clap,
clap!

happy. So she sang,

If you're happy and you know it,

and you really want to show it...

If you're happy and you know it, whisk your tail around to show it.

If you're happy and you know it,
wag your tail!'

'My tail is rather insignificant,'
said the elephant. 'So I sing,

If you're happy and you know it,
flap your ears.
If you're happy and you know it,
flap your ears –

flip,   flap!

If you're happy and you know it,

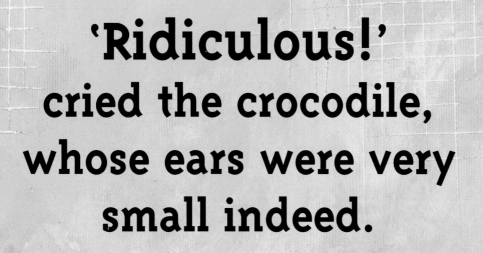

'Ridiculous!'
cried the crocodile,
whose ears were very
small indeed.

'If you're happy and you
know it, snap your teeth.

If you're happy and you know it, snap

'Pathetic,'
said the gorilla.

'If you're happy and you know it,
beat your chest.

If you're happy
and you know it,
pound your chest –
boom, boom!
If you're happy
and you know it,

boing boing along
to show it!'

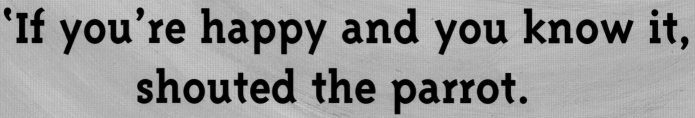

'If you're happy and you know it, shouted the parrot.

'If you're happy and you know it, you should

ya

you should **screech!**

scream –
hoo!

If you're happy
and you know it,

shriek
and shrill,

scream
and yell.

If you're happy
and you know it,
you should screech.

The hyena giggled.

'If you're happy and you know it, have a laugh.

If you're happy and you know it, say tee-hee, ha-ha, ho-ho!

If you're tickled and you know it,
chortle, cackle, chuckle, titter.
If you're happy and you know it,
have a tee hee hee.

'So when I'm happy,' laughed the little girl, 'I can do my own thing!'

'That's right,' they all cried.

you know it, do your thing.
you know it, smile and grin.
flap your ears,
snap your teeth,
boom boing.
thing
HOO!

'Doing the Animal Bop' can be sung to any sort of jazzy rhythm – it makes a great calypso or rap, for example! This song is all about expression: the noises animals make and the ways they move. Children will love imitating different animal sounds – and there are lots to copy. And don't forget the mouse! He appears on every spread: so why not ask your child to squeak and scurry, just like the tiniest little mouse?

Doing the Animal
BOP

IF you like to **dance**
and you sometimes **sing,**

why don't
you do the
animal thing?

Put your heels together,

and Waddle along.

High stepping knees
and feathers that
bounce-

flim - flam
flutter
to the **ostrich** flounce.

Jump and wiggle
to the monkey bop.

Kick
those legs
like the **donkeys** do.

Then go
hee-haw
hee-
haw, too!

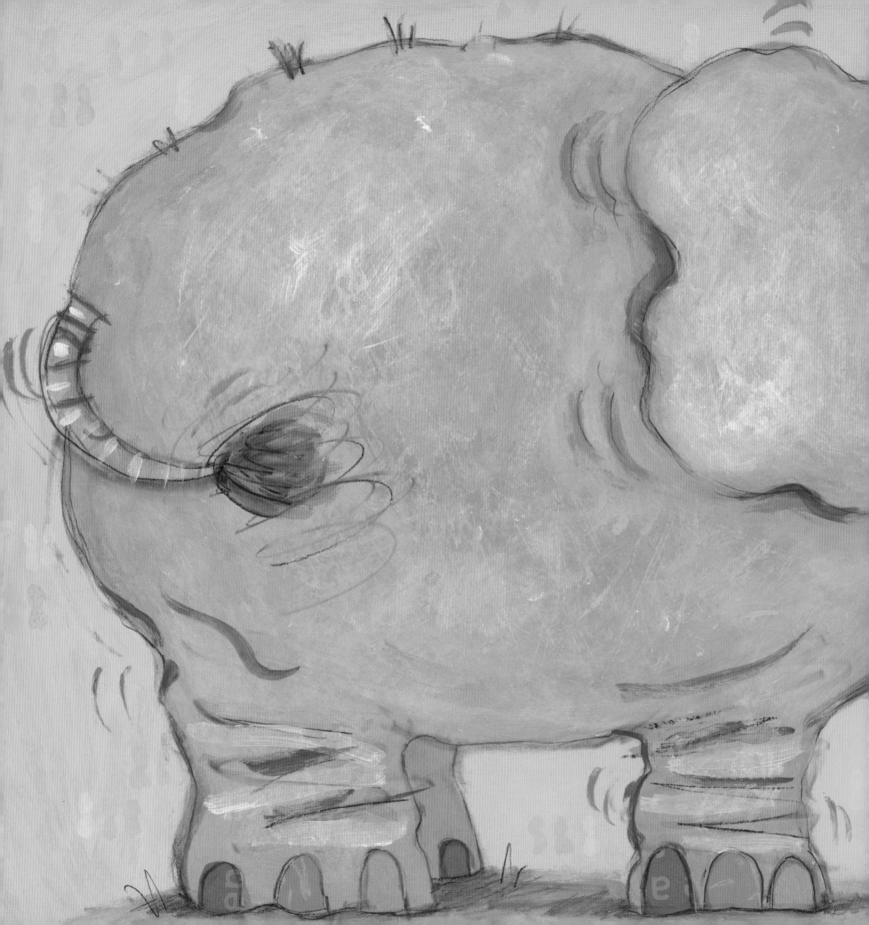

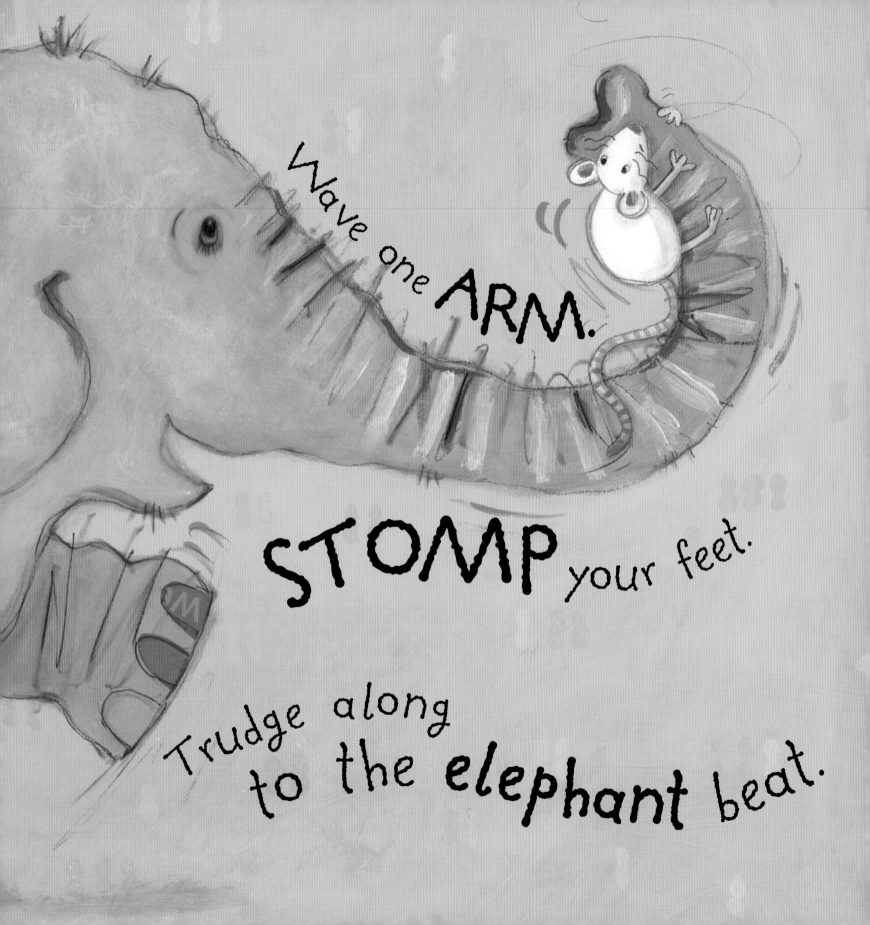

Wave one ARM.

STOMP your feet.

Trudge along to the elephant beat.

Move **one** leg.

Now move **two** . . .

. . . move the way that the **lizards** do.

A chicken can **peck** . . .

. . . and a chicken can CLUCK.

But I think it's more fun
being a **duck** . . .

The duck does a **waddle**

on his **FLIP-FLAP** feet,

so **swing** your bottom

to the
quack-quack beat.

Roar and rage,

it's a rhino romp!

All the **COW** can do is chew.